S0-BDH-272

Hooray for Our Heroes!

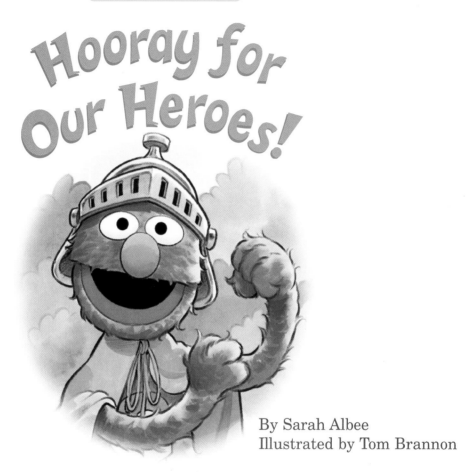

By Sarah Albee
Illustrated by Tom Brannon

Dalmatian Press, LLC, 2008. All rights reserved.
Published by Dalmatian Press, LLC, 2008. The DALMATIAN PRESS name and logo are trademarks of Dalmatian Press, LLC, Franklin, Tennessee 37067. No part of this book may be reproduced or copied in any form without written permission from the copyright owner.

Printed in the U.S.A.
ISBN: 1-40374-188-3

07 08 09 10 NGS 10 9 8 7 6 5 4 3 2 1
15225 Sesame Street 8x8 Storybook: Hooray for Our Heroes!

Hello there, everybodee! It is I, your furry superhero pal, Super Grover! Today I am going to tell you what the word "hero" means. A hero is someone who you see in comic books and cartoons. Heroes are make-believe.

First of all, a hero has a special uniform, similar to the outfit that I am wearing, with a cape on the back and a letter on the chest. I do not see anyone else wearing a hero uniform, do you?

And, of course, everyone knows that heroes have very large muscles and are very strong. No one around *here* is especially strong.

Heroes move with lightning speed. No one around *here* can do that.

Of course, heroes must also be able to fly. Aside from yours truly, no one around *here* can do that.

And heroes must be able to leap tall buildings in a single bound.

Heroes are famous. They are never the people that we see walking around our own neighborhoods.

How would you know a hero if you saw one? That is a very good question! And I, Grover, will answer it for you. For starters, heroes definitely do not wear glasses.

And heroes do not just sit around, waiting for things to happen.

Heroes rescue people who need help. I do not see anyone around here being rescued, do you?

Heroes are people you look up to.

I hope that now you understand what it means to be a hero. Thank you!